Aladdin and the Magic Lamp

Retold by Jordan Horowitz • Illustrated by Joe Boddy

ISBN 0-590-46417-5

12 11 10 9 8 7 6 5 4 3 3 4 5 6 7/9

Printed in the U.S.A. 24

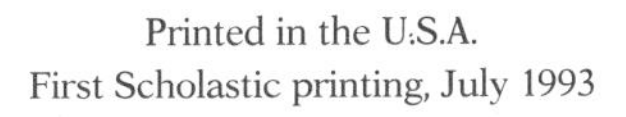

First Scholastic printing, July 1993

SCHOLASTIC INC.
New York Toronto London Auckland Sydney

Long ago, and far away, there lived a young man named Aladdin. Aladdin's father had died without ever teaching him a trade. Now he had no skills and could not earn a living.

Every day Aladdin had to go to the marketplace to beg for food so that he and his mother would not go hungry.

Then one day, Aladdin met an old magician. "Come with me," said the magician. "I will teach you magic."

The magician led Aladdin to the entrance of a cave. "Go inside the cave and look for an old, tarnished lamp," the magician told Aladdin. "When you find it, bring it to me."

Aladdin peeked inside the cave. It seemed dark and gloomy.

"If you go into the cave you may keep all the treasure you find there," said the magician.

"But I am frightened," Aladdin whispered to the magician.

"Nonsense," said the magician. He placed a magic ring on Aladdin's finger. "This ring will protect you from all harm," he said. "Go now!"

The ring made Aladdin feel brave. He took a deep breath and entered the cave. Much to his surprise, it wasn't dark inside the cave at all. The cave was filled with glittering treasure!

Aladdin saw the old, tarnished lamp sitting on a ledge. He removed it just as he had been told. Then he hurried to fill his pockets with as much treasure as they could hold.

“Magician,” called Aladdin. “I have the lamp!”

“Pass the lamp to me at once!” commanded the magician.

“Help me out of the cave,” cried Aladdin. “My pockets are filled with treasure. I am too heavy. I cannot move!”

The magician didn’t care about Aladdin. All he wanted was the lamp.

“First pass me the lamp,” demanded the magician. “Then I will help you out.”

But Aladdin refused.

The magician became very angry. He sprinkled incense and hurled a magic charm. At once, dirt rose up from the ground and blocked the entrance to the cave.

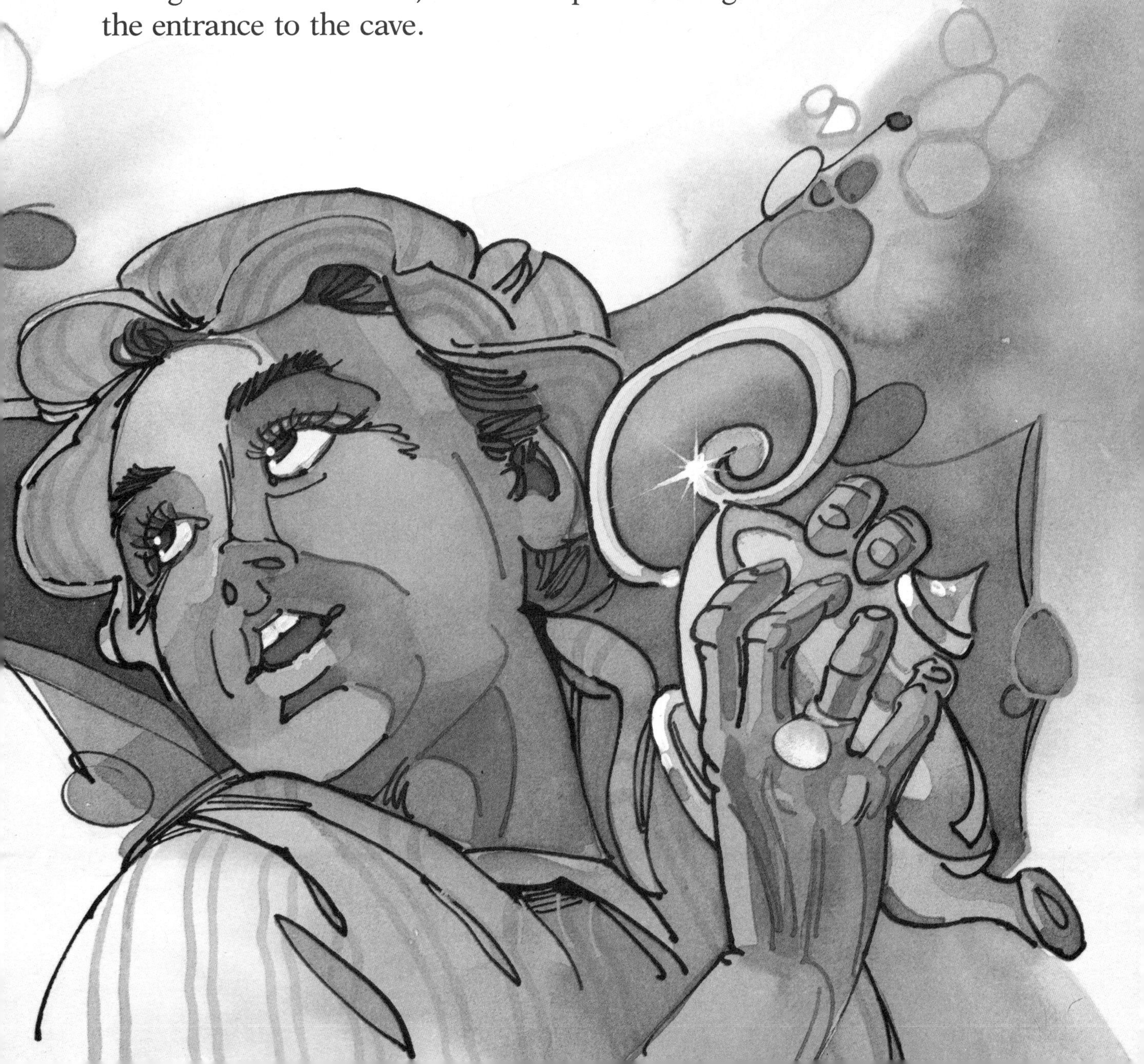

Frantically, Aladdin emptied his pockets of treasure and tried to dig his way out of the cave. But the dirt was too deep. Aladdin rubbed his hands in despair. In so doing, he rubbed the magic ring the magician had placed on his finger.

Suddenly, a genie rose out of the ring and stood before him.

"I am the Genie of the Ring," he said. "Wish for anything and I shall grant it!"

"I wish to be taken home to my mother," said Aladdin.

"Your wish is my command!" replied the genie.

And it was done.

The next day Aladdin was very hungry, but he had no money to buy any food.

Then he had an idea. He took out the old lamp which he had taken from the cave and began to polish it.

"I will polish this lamp until it is shiny and new," he said. "Then I can sell it and use the money to buy food."

Suddenly another genie appeared before him.
"I am the Genie of the Lamp," he said. "Wish for anything and I will grant it!"
"Make me a feast of the tastiest quail eggs and the sweetest fruits," said Aladdin.
"I hear and I obey," said the genie.
And it was done.

The very next day, Aladdin was in the marketplace. There he met the royal princess.

They fell instantly in love.

Aladdin went to her father, the Sultan, and asked for her hand in marriage. But the Sultan had already promised his daughter to the son of his most trusted advisor.

The princess did not like the old man's son. She had already promised her heart to Aladdin. The Sultan was not sure what to do.

"Command Aladdin to bring forty casks of treasure to prove his love," said the Sultan's advisor. "That young upstart will never be able to find such a sum."

And that is what the Sultan did.

At first, Aladdin was sad. Where would he find forty casks of treasure?

Then he remembered that he had something no other man in the kingdom had. He had a magic lamp.

Quickly he rubbed the lamp and summoned the genie.

"Wish for anything and I shall grant it," said the genie.
"I wish for forty casks of treasure," said Aladdin.
"I hear and I obey," replied the genie.
And it was done.

That very evening, Aladdin presented the casks of treasure to the Sultan.

When the Sultan saw all the treasure he was overjoyed. "Aladdin," he said. "You have shown yourself worthy to marry my daughter."

The next day there was a big wedding feast. Everyone in the kingdom danced and rejoiced. They gave Aladdin and his bride gifts of all shapes, sizes, and colors. Aladdin could not believe his good fortune.

Soon word of Aladdin's happiness reached the ears of the old magician. He knew the Genie of the Lamp had helped Aladdin win the hand of the princess, and he was jealous. He decided on a trick to get the lamp for himself!

The magician disguised himself as a trader of lamps. Then he went to the palace. "Old lamps for new!" he called out. "I'm trading old lamps for new!"

The princess did not know that Aladdin's lamp was magic. *What would Aladdin want with such an old lamp?* she thought. *I will surprise him and trade it for a shiny new one.*

And so, the princess invited the magician into the palace. She gave him Aladdin's lamp.

Quickly the magician rubbed the lamp.

The genie appeared.

"Carry this palace and everyone in it to my home, far, far away," commanded the magician.

"I hear and I obey," replied the genie unhappily.

And it was done.

When Aladdin returned home the palace and the princess had vanished! Aladdin was afraid for the princess's safety. He wrung his hands together in gloom.

And in so doing, he once again rubbed his magic ring. At once the Genie of the Ring appeared and told Aladdin all that had happened.

"Return the palace and the princess to me," said Aladdin.

"Alas," replied the genie. "I cannot undo what another genie has done."

"Then send me to the princess and I will rescue her," Aladdin ordered.

And so it was done.

Aladdin found the princess. He heaved a heavy sigh of relief when he saw that she was safe.

He hugged her tight.

Together they promised never to be separated again.

When he saw Aladdin, the magician was so surprised that he dropped the magic lamp from his hands.

Aladdin caught the lamp and summoned the genie. "Send this evil magician away forever!" he said to the Genie of the Lamp.

"I hear and I obey," said the genie happily. A great wind came and took the magician away.

"Return this palace and everyone in it," Aladdin ordered.

"Your wish is my command," smiled the genie.

And it was done.

Aladdin and the princess soon had a child, and they all lived happily ever after.